Judy Moo
The Doctor Is In!

Megan McDonald is the award-winning author
of the Judy Moody series. She says that most
of Judy's stories "grew out of anecdotes about
growing up with my four sisters". She confesses,
"I am Judy Moody. Same-same! In my family
of sisters, we're famous for exaggeration. Judy
Moody is me … exaggerated." Megan McDonald
lives with her husband in northern California.

You can find out more about Megan McDonald
and her books at **www.meganmcdonald.net**

Peter H. Reynolds says he felt an immediate
connection to Judy Moody because "having
a daughter, I have witnessed first-hand the
adventures of a very independent-minded girl".
Peter H. Reynolds lives in Massachusetts, just
down the road from his twin brother.

You can find out more about Peter H. Reynolds
and his art at **www.fablevision.com**

Judy Moody
The Doctor Is In!

Megan McDonald

illustrated by

Peter H. Reynolds

WALKER
BOOKS

First published 2004 by Walker Books Ltd
87 Vauxhall Walk, London SE11 5HJ

This edition published 2011

35

Text © 2004 Megan McDonald
Illustrations © 2004 Peter H. Reynolds
Judy Moody font © 2003 Peter H. Reynolds

This book has been typeset in Stone Informal

Printed and bound in Great Britain by Clays Ltd, St Ives plc

British Library Cataloguing in Publication Data:
a catalogue record for this book
is available from the British Library

ISBN 978-1-4063-3586-6

www.walker.co.uk

For my editor, Mary Lee Donovan,
who cheerfully helps with Moody Days,
Multiple Deadlines, Melt-Downs,
and other Mega-Disasters.
M.M.

To Maribeth Bush, whose "can do"
spirit inspires so many!
P.H.R.

Table of Contents

Judy

First Girl Doctor

Who's

Dad

Father of Mumpty
Dumpty

Mum

Nurse-in-residence

Mouse

Cool critter

Stink

Organ donor

Who

Toady

Guinea pig?

Rocky

Judy's new
un-best friend

Mr Todd

For pencil emergencies,
dial Mr Todd

Frank

Gene-ius

Jessica

Diagnosis:
microbes on the *medulla*

A Moody Day

PLIP! Judy Moody woke up. *Drip, drip, drip* went rain on the roof. *Blip, blip, blip* went drops on the window. Not again! It had been raining for seven days straight. Bor-ing!

She, Judy Moody, was sick and tired of rain.

Judy put her head under the pillow. If only she was sick. Being sick was the greatest. You got to stay home and drink pop for breakfast and eat toast cut in special strips and watch TV in your room. You got to read Cherry Ames, Student Nurse, mysteries all day. And you got to eat yummy cherry cough drops. Hey! Maybe Cherry Ames was named after a cough drop!

Judy took out her mum's old Cherry Ames book and popped a cough drop in her mouth anyway.

"Get up, Lazybones!" said Stink, knocking on her door.

"Can't," said Judy. "Too much rain."

"What?"

"Never mind. Just go to school without me."

"Mum, Judy's skipping school!" Stink yelled.

Mum came into Judy's room. "Judy, honey. What's wrong?"

"I'm sick. Of *rain*," she whispered to Mouse.

"Sick? What's wrong? What hurts?" asked Mum.

"My head, for one thing. From all that noisy rain."

"You have a headache?"

"Yes. And a sore throat. And a fever. And a stiff neck."

"That's from sleeping with the dictionary under your pillow," said Stink. "To ace your spelling test."

"Is not."

"Is too!"

"See, look. My tongue's all red." Judy

stuck out her Cherry-Ames-cough-drop tongue at Stink.

Mum felt Judy's forehead. "You don't seem to have a fever."

"Faker," said Stink.

"Come back in five minutes," said Judy. "I'll have a fever by then."

"Faker, faker, faker," said Stink.

If only she had measles. Or chicken-pox. Or ... MUMPS! Mumps gave you a headache. Mumps gave you a stiff neck and a sore throat. Mumps made your cheeks stick out like Humpty Dumpty. Judy pushed the cough drop into her cheek and made it stick out, Humpty-Dumpty style.

"Mumps!" said Dr Judy. "I think I have the mumps! For real!"

"Mumps!" said Stink. "No way. You got a shot for that. A no-mumps shot. We both did. Didn't we, Mum?"

"Yes," said Mum. "Stink's right."

"Maybe one mump got through."

"Sounds like somebody doesn't want to go to school today," said Mum.

"Can I? Can I stay home, Mum? I promise I'll be sick. All day."

"Let's take your temperature," said Mum. She took the thermometer out of the case.

"Cat hair?" said Mum. "Is this cat hair on the thermometer?"

"She's always making Mouse stick out her tongue and taking the cat's temperature," said Stink.

Mum shook her head and went to wash off the thermometer. When she came back, she took Judy's temperature. "It's 98.6," said Mum. "Normal!"

"Faker, fakey, not-sick, big fat faker," said Stink.

"At least my temperature's normal," said Judy. "Even if my brother isn't."

"Better get dressed," said Mum. "Don't want to be late."

"Stink? You're a rat fink. Stink Rat-Fink Moody. That's what I'll call you from now on."

"Well, you'll have to call me it at school, cos you don't get to stay home."

Judy stuck out her cherry-red, no-mumps tongue at Stink.

She was down in the dumps. She had a bad case of the grumps. The no-mumps Moody Monday blues. She, Judy Moody, felt like Mumpty Dumpty! Mumpty Dumpty without a temperature, that is.

Medullas and Mandibles

When Judy walked into Class 3T (seven minutes late!) on the un-mumpsy day of Monday, Class 3T was dry as a bone. Or bones! There were bones everywhere.

Mr Todd had made a new bulletin board: *Our Amazing Body: From Head to Toe.* It had a tall poster of bones with long scientific names. On the front board he taped a chart that showed rodent bones. It looked like the insides of Peanut, the dwarf guinea pig in Class 3T. And ... sitting behind Mr Todd's desk in Mr Todd's chair, using Mr Todd's pencil, was a glow-in-the-dark skeleton!

Class 3T had turned into a bone museum!

Bones were not drippy. Bones were not noisy. Bones were not boring. Bones were dry and quiet and very, very interesting!

Things were sure looking up for a no-mumps Monday. Judy handed Mr Todd her late pass. "Sorry I'm late," she said. "I almost had the mumps."

"Well, I'm glad you're healthy, and here now. We're starting a new project on the human body from head to toe."

"We're going to do some skipping,"

said Jessica Finch. "And measure our heart rates."

"And play Twister," said Rocky. "To learn about muscles." .

"And sing a song about bones," said Alison S.

"I can't believe you started the human body without me!" said Judy. "A person can miss a lot in seven minutes."

"Don't worry. I think you'll catch up," said Mr Todd.

Mr Todd taught them a funny song that went, "Da foot bone's connected to da ankle bone..." He read them a book called *Frozen Man*, the incredible, real-life story of a five-thousand-year-old mummy.

And Class 3T got to turn out the lights and use the glow-in-the-dark skeleton named Bonita to count how many bones were in a human. Two hundred and six!

"We'll be learning a lot of new words in this unit. The scientific names for bones and body parts come from Latin. So they may sound a little funny."

"Like *maxilla* is your jaw?" asked Judy, looking at the bulletin board.

"And so is *mandible*," said Jessica.

Jessica Finch had already learnt to spell *microbes* (a fancy word for germs, as in cooties!) and *medulla* (a fancy word for brain stuff). "Can you spell *headache*?" Judy asked. Frank Pearl cracked up at that one.

Then Mr Todd passed out owl pellets. They got to poke them with a pencil to find bones. Rodent bones. Judy and Frank stared at their fuzzy grey lump.

"Double bluck! Just think. This is owl vomit!" said Frank.

"It's still interesting," said Judy. "Real bones are in there. Skulls and stuff."

"You poke it," said Frank. So Judy poked it with her Grouchy pencil. They found a jawbone, a rib and a bone Mr Todd called a *femur*. They glued each bone onto paper and drew in all the missing bones to make a rodent skeleton that matched the one on the board.

"Do any rodent bones have the same names as human bones?" asked Mr Todd.

Judy raised her hand.

"Tibia," called out Jessica Finch.

"Very good," said Mr Todd.

"That's what I was going to say," said Judy. Jessica Finch was a rat fink (like Stink!) for not raising her hand. A *rodent* fink.

"Now let's talk about your Human Body projects," said Mr Todd. "Projects will be due in two weeks. You can do your project on bones, muscles, joints, the brain—"

"Even toe nails?" asked Brad.

"As long as it teaches us something about the human body. Let's start by writing down ideas in your notebooks. I want to see brainstorming."

☐ Do an operation (on Toady?)
☐ Dress up and be Elizabeth Blackwell (first Woman Doctor)
☐ Tell doctor jokes about body parts
☐ Show and Tell a body Part (from scab Collection)
☐ Listen to heartbeat with stethoscope

Judy had a storm in her brain already.

Rocky wanted to do three-thousand-year-old human body stuff. Mummies!

"What are you thinking of doing?" Judy asked Frank.

"Cloning. I'll be a fiction scientist, or a science fictiontist. Somebody who clones stuff. Like in *Jurassic Park*. They used a drop of mosquito blood and made a whole dinosaur. They do it in real life too. Start with one cell, like from your DNA, and make a whole new you."

"*Double* cool!" Judy said.

"I'm going to write a dictionary," Jessica told Judy. "With human body words like *appendix* and *patella*. That's your knee." Jessica Finch had *microbes* on the *medulla* if she thought she could rewrite the dictionary.

Judy looked back at her own paper. She chewed her eraser. She chewed her fingernail. She chewed her hair. Judy had a brainwave! A real-body-parts idea. She would call Grandma Lou to see if she had any good body parts for Showing and Telling. Something better than scabs. This was the brainiest of all storms! She wrote down *Call Grandma Lou* so she wouldn't forget.

Judy's just-sharpened Grouchy pencil was still flying when Mr Todd said, "Class, that's enough brainstorming for today."

"Good. My brain hurts," said Frank.

"I'm passing out permission slips for our field trip."

Field trip! "Is it to Screamin' Mimi's?" asked Judy. "Please, please, pretty please with Chocolate Mud ice cream on top?"

"Max and Kelsey's dad, from Class 3M, works at the hospital. So we're invited to go with their class to County General A&E Department. We'll learn all about the human body and get to see people who make a difference *in action.*"

Accident and Emergency! That was even better than Screamin' Mimi's! Judy Moody dropped her *mandible!* And her Grouchy pencil.

"I was there when I broke my finger," said Frank, waving his crooked pinkie.

"They have a nurse named Ron."

"I went when my brother stuck a piece of Lego up his nose," said Brad.

"Can we go see all the new babies?" asked Frank. "They're so wrinkly."

"Well, I'm glad the whole class is enthusiastic," said Mr Todd.

"When do we go? When? When?" everybody asked.

"Monday. One week from today. Dr Nosier will be giving us a tour."

"Dr Nosehair!" said Rocky, and everybody cracked up.

She, Judy Moody, and Class 3T were going to A&E. For real and absolute positive. The blood-and-guts, real-body-parts A&E Department.

Judy reached down to pick up her Grouchy pencil. The tip was broken. "Mr Todd," she asked, "may I please sharpen my pencil?"

"Remember what we said about sharpening pencils ten times a day?"

"But Mr Todd," said Judy, "it's an emergency."

"What?"

"A *pencil* emergency! My pencil just broke its spinal cord!" said Judy.

Mystery Detective

The next Monday was a better-than-best-ever third grade day. At lunch, Judy ate her peanut butter and jam sandwich in seven bites, then walked-not-ran to the playground. Class 3T had a ten-minute recess before their trip to the hospital.

Judy's mum was a driver and parent volunteer, so Rocky and Frank rode in their car. Mum made Judy ask Jessica Finch too.

"Did you know *muscle* comes from a

word that means mouse?" asked Jessica. "If you move a muscle, it looks like a mouse." She flexed her arm.

Judy used all forty-three muscles it took to frown at Jessica Finch.

◎   ◎   ◎

At the hospital, Dr Nosehair led Class 3T down a long hall.

"Why does that doctor lady have a rabbit?" asked Frank.

"Animals aren't allowed in the hospital!" said Jessica.

"It's a new programme called Paws for Healing," Dr Nosier told them. "People bring animals to patients in the hospital to help them feel better. Holding an animal and petting it can actually lower a person's blood pressure, and help a patient forget about being sick."

"RARE!" said Judy.

Dr N. took them into a room at the back of A&E, where Class 3M was already waiting. There were lots of machines. And important-looking stuff.

"What's the first thing you would do in an emergency?" quizzed Dr Nosier.

"Call 999!" everybody said.

"Would you call 999 to find out how long to cook a turkey?"

"Only if *you're* a turkey," Frank said. Judy and Frank cracked up.

"Is a crossword puzzle an emergency?"

"Only for my dad, who tries to beat the clock," said Judy.

"Believe it or not, we do get people who call 999 for such things. But let's say we have a real emergency, like a car accident or a heart attack. Everything around here happens super fast. As soon as the ambulance arrives, the paramedics, people trained to handle medical emergencies, start 'giving the bullet' – telling us what happened. *Train wreck* means the patient has lots of things wrong with them. Who knows what *code blue* means?"

"Lots of blood?"

"All the people in blue shirts have to help?"

"It means somebody's heart stopped," said Dr Nosier.

"You fix hearts that stop?" asked Alison S.

"You must help a lot of people!" said Erica.

"All doctors make a promise to help people. It's called the Hippocratic oath. Hippocrates was the Father of Medicine. In the old days, you had to swear by Apollo and Hygeia to help people the best you could. If you didn't know what was wrong with a patient, you had to say 'I know not'. The old oath sounds funny to us now, so a doctor named Louis Lasagna rewrote it."

"Louis *Lasagna*? Did he invent pizza too?" asked Frank. Dr N. laughed.

"But how do you always know what to do?" asked Rocky.

"Being a doctor is like being a detective. You look at all the clues and try to solve the mystery. In A&E we just do it in a hurry. Think of it like each one of us is a human jigsaw puzzle. My job is to figure out the missing pieces and put the puzzle back together."

"RARE!" whispered Judy.

"I'm the best at jigsaw puzzles," bragged Jessica Finch. "I did a five-hundred-piece jigsaw puzzle of Big Ben all by myself!" Sometimes Judy wished Jessica Finch would shut her *mandible*.

"Now I'll show you what some of this stuff is for," said Dr Nosier. Dr Judy got to use a stethoscope to listen to her own heartbeat! *Ba-boom, ba-boom!* Then she took Frank's blood pressure (for real!), looked for Jessica Finch's tonsils, and saw eye insides with a special kind of scope. They took turns riding on a trolley, walking with crutches and sitting in a wheelchair.

Dr N. turned out all the lights and showed them X-rays. There was a brain (it looked all ghosty), a dog that got hit by a car (it looked all sideways), even a violin (it looked all dead!). "X-rays help solve the mystery," he said.

They even got to see a real live, ooey-gooey heart on a TV. "This is better than the Operation Channel at home!" Judy said.

And they got to practise on life-size dummies called Hurt-Head Harry and Trauma Tammy. "I have a practice doll too," said Judy. "With three heads. Hedda-Get-Betta. I practise being a doctor, like Elizabeth Blackwell."

"How would you like to practise being a patient with a broken arm?" asked Dr N. "And I'll show everybody how we put on a cast."

Judy Moody could not believe her inner, middle or outer ears. "Can I, Mum?"

"Sure, if you want to."

"Hold out your arm, Judy Moody, First Girl Doctor."

Judy grinned with all seventeen muscles it takes to make a smile. She held her arm out straight as a snowman's stick-arm. Dr N. wrapped it round and round with soft cotton stuff.

"I'll use a special plaster bandage that turns hard when it dries so Judy won't be able to move that arm. That way her bone will stay in place and heal back together."

"My *radius* or my *ulna*?" asked Judy.

"I see you know your bones! Can you still wiggle your *phalanges*?"

Judy wiggled her fingers. Everybody laughed.

"A not-broken arm is even better than

a broken arm! I wish I never had to take it off."

"Tell you what," said Dr Nosier. "If your mum says it's OK, you can wear it home. I'll show her how to take it off."

"Can I, Mum? Can I? I can trick Stink! Please, pretty please with Band-Aids on top?"

"I don't see why not," said Mum. "Sure!"

"RARE!" said Judy. She, Judy Moody, was a mystery. A human jigsaw puzzle with a broken arm ... NOT!

Judy was so happy from Hospital Day that even her eyebrows were smiling. She stared at all the signatures on her cast. Even Dr Nosehair had signed it. His

signature looked like a messy blob, but still! She could hardly wait to get home and show Dad her cast. Maybe she could even get out of setting the table, on account of her broken arm (not!). Wait till she told Stink!

When she got home, Stink was waiting at the front door. Judy held up her cast.

"You broke your arm?" asked Stink. "Sweet!"

A Million Dollars

She, Judy Moody, was in an operating mood! As soon as she got her cast off, Judy asked Stink to play Operation, a game where you remove body parts with tweezers and try NOT to make the buzzer go off.

Dr Judy performed a delicate operation and removed butterflies from the patient's stomach. Next she removed his broken heart. Stink went for the charley horse.

Buzz! "Hey, his nose lights up red," he said. "Like Rudolph the Red-Nosed Reindeer!"

"You did that on purpose!"

"Did not!" Stink tried to remove the pencil from the guy's arm, to get rid of writer's cramp. *Buzz! Buzz! Buzz!*

"Stink. Give me the tweezers. Your turn's over when you buzz."

"Let's play something else," said Stink.

"I know," Judy said. "You can help me with my Human Body project for school."

"That's not playing. That's homework."

"*Fun* homework," said Judy. "I'm going to do an operation with real stitches and stuff." Judy got out her doctor kit. "All I need is somebody to operate on."

"You're not operating on me. Just so you

know. No slings or eye patches or anything."

"Can I at least take your blood pressure?"

"I guess."

Judy put a cuff round Stink's arm and pumped air into it. "I'm afraid you have high blood pressure, Stink," said Judy. "Your heart's beating super fast."

"That's cos I'm scared of what you might do to me!"

"I have a better idea." Judy went straight to Toady's aquarium. "Operation Toady! You hold him down, Stink, and I'll make the incision."

"The what?"

"The cut. Hel-lo? It's an *oper-a-tion*."

"You're loony tunes!" Stink said. "You can't cut Toady open."

"I'll stitch him back up. C'mon. Just one small, teensy-weensy snip?"

"N-O, no! Give him to me!"

"It's the only way to see toad insides. Admit it, Stink. You want to see toad guts."

"Not *this* toad's guts." Stink rushed over to his desk and rooted around in the top drawer. He held up a cardboard badge that said RSPCA: SAVING LIVES SINCE 1824. "Busted!" said Stink, holding the badge up to Judy's face. "It's against the law to be mean to animals or hurt them. Ever. Just show them respect and kindness. You're not even supposed to let your dog drink out of the toilet."

"I don't have a dog. And Mouse doesn't drink out of the toilet!"

"Good. If she did, you'd go to jail."

"I was just going to practise on Toady. Not put him in the toilet!"

"You're not allowed to test stuff out on animals. You're supposed to test on beans. Or pumpkins. People who make soap and shampoo and underpants and stuff are always testing it on animals, and the animals get hurt or even die."

"Stink, nobody makes animals wear underpants."

"Yah-huh. They do. No lie. It makes me really sad and mad that people do stuff to animals. I'm so sad and so mad I'm … smad!"

"OK, OK! Don't be smad. I cross-my-heart promise I won't shampoo Toady or

make him wear underpants or anything.
I just wish I had something really good
for Sharing. Something
nobody's ever seen.
Something *human*."

"Like what?"

"Like Einstein's brain.
A hair from Abraham Lincoln's beard.
Or Grandma Lou's kidney stone, if only
she had saved it."

"Put a kidney bean in a jar and say
it's Einstein's brain. You could say it's a
human bean, get it?"

"Hardee-har-har, Stink."

"I have some baby teeth. Teeth are
human."

"Everybody's seen baby teeth, Stink."

"I have a toe nail collection."

"Bor-ing."

"Wait! I *do* have a body part."

"What? What is it? Can I have it?"

"Nope. I'm not showing you, cos you'll want it bad."

"Is it a finger? Or an ear?"

"NO!"

"A bone?"

"Nope."

"Is it skin? Like you peel off when you get sunburnt?"

"Nope."

"Is it a cavity? You know, like in a tooth?"

"Nope."

"C'mon, Stinker. You HAVE to show me."

"OK, but promise you won't SHOW or TELL anybody, and you can't take it to school, OK?"

"Cross-my-heart promise," said Judy.

Stink went over to his closet. He pulled down a dusty box from the shelf. A box with all his baby stuff.

"Hurry up. I can't stand it!" said Judy.

Stink opened the box and took out a baby-food jar. There was something in the jar. Something that looked like a shrivelled-up, shrunken dead worm.

"Yee-uck. What is it? A petrified worm? Or one-hundred-year-old burnt spaghetti?"

"No, Einstein. It's my belly button!"

"Your belly button?"

"You know. That thing that falls off your belly button when you're born."

"For real and true?"

"Yes, for real. When Mum brought me home from the hospital—"

"But you were born in a Jeep!"

"You know what I mean. When I came home, I had a thing on my belly button. You have to wait for it to fall off. Mum said you wanted to keep it."

"Me? So, then, really it's mine?"

"NO! It's *my* body part. I used to be an outie. Now I'm an innie." Stink lifted up his shirt. "See?"

"RARE!" said Judy. "I can't wait for my class" – Stink gave her a starey, glarey look – "to NOT know about this. Ever."

Stink put the jar with his wormy old burnt-spaghetti belly button on the desk. "You know what's so great about this belly button?"

"What?" asked Judy.

"That you don't have one!" said Stink. He laughed himself silly. "But if you give me a million dollars, I'll let you take my belly button to school."

"How about five dollars?"

"A million dollars or you'll never, not ever, touch my belly button!" said Stink.

Mucus Dermis

Wednesday. Wednesday was her Sharing Day! Judy was going to have the best share ever. She couldn't wait until her Human Body project was due. She, Judy Moody, would Show and Tell about Stink's belly button. Today. All she had to do was steal it.

Judy waited for Stink to go downstairs for breakfast. She tiptoed into his room, took down the box of baby stuff, grabbed

Stink's belly-button jar, and hid it in the secret inside pocket of her backpack.

☙   ☙   ☙

As soon as the bell rang, Mr Todd asked Class 3T to form a Sharing Circle. It was Rocky's day to share too. And Jessica Finch. Jessica said she'd brought an especially special share. But Judy just knew her belly button had to be the special-est!

Rocky went first. His share was a piece of Lego. Judy thought one piece of Lego was boring, until Rocky conducted an experiment on it. He put it in a Petri dish and poured some stuff on it. The Lego turned black-as-dirt from all the germs on it.

"Eee-yew!" said Jessica Finch. "Germs!" Germs made her squirm.

"There's a fungus among us," said Frank.

"I had lice before," said Brad. "In my hair!"

"Me too!" said Alison S.

"Ick," said Dylan, backing away from the circle.

"Millions of bacteria are on us all the time," said Rocky. "On our heads, up our noses, between our toes."

"That's right," said Mr Todd. "Each one of us is our own ecosystem. We carry around millions of creatures too tiny to see."

"Like a human rainforest?" asked Judy.

"Exactly," said Mr Todd. "Now do you see why I'm always after all of you to wash your hands?"

"I have something that's not germs,"
Jessica said. "My guinea pig, Chester, was
a boy, but he turned out to be a girl and
had babies." Jessica Finch held up a picture.
"Nutmeg, Jasmine, Coco and Cindy, short
for Cinnamon. The Spice Girls!"

"Ahh!" everybody said. "Cute!"

Judy took a look. All she could see were hair balls. Belly buttons were way more scientific than hair balls!

"Judy, did you bring anything to share?" asked Mr Todd.

"Yes," said Judy. She held the baby-food jar behind her back. "See, when you're a baby and you first come out, there's a thingy attached to your belly button. Then it falls off and your mum and dad find out if you're an innie or an outie."

"I'm an innie!" said Frank.

"Ooh. I'm a way-outie!" said Brad, showing off his belly button.

"OK, 3T! Keep your shirts on," said Mr Todd. "Let's let Judy finish."

"In this jar, I have a real live belly-button thingy. No lie. I call it *Mucus Dermis*. It's Latin. *Dermis* means skin and *mucus* means yucky. Yucky skin."

"Where'd you get it?" asked Rocky.

"Actually, it's from my very own brother, Stink Moody."

"Double yuck," said Jessica Finch, squirming in a wormy way.

"Let me see!" said Frank Pearl. Judy passed Stink's belly button to Frank. Everybody crowded round to see.

"Take your seats and Judy will pass it around," said Mr Todd.

"Belly buttons are also called navels," said Judy. "Everybody has one, but no two are alike. Just like snowflakes. Sometimes belly buttons collect lint, and in Japan they have belly-button cleaners. My dad told me. No lie!"

"Thank you, Judy," said Mr Todd. "I think we've all learnt more than we ever imagined about belly buttons."

"Belly buttons are better than bones," said Rocky.

"Better than lice!" said Frank.

"Better than hair balls!" said Judy.

"Does your brother know you have his belly button?" asked Jessica.

Mr Dry-Bones

After Sharing, Judy went out in the hall to put away her backpack. Stink was there, listening right outside the classroom.

"Give it," said Stink, holding out his hand.

"Give what?"

"I know you have it. I came to tell you ... I just saw you! I overheard... You stole it, didn't you? You showed the WHOLE ENTIRE WORLD my belly button!"

"Nah-uh! Only half of the third grade."

"You owe me a million dollars."

"Stink, we can fight later. Go back to second grade."

"I can't. I'm sick. My throat hurts. I think I have mumps."

"Made-up mumps?"

"No. For real." Stink held his neck like it really hurt.

"Would you say that the pain is in your *larynx* or your *pharynx*?" Judy asked.

"Huh?"

"Just go to the nurse," said Judy.

"I'm scared."

"Of what? Mrs Bell?"

"No."

"A shot?"

"No."

"Getting lost?"

"No."

"For-real mumps? A pill? Throwing up?"

"No. No. And not really."

"What? What are you scared of?"

"The skeleton! In the nurse's office."

"Stink! It's not even real!"

Stink's face crumpled like he was going to cry. "The office lady told me to wait till Mrs Bell gets here, but I was in there all by myself. With *it*."

"I'll take you, if you promise not to be mad about the belly button."

Judy got a pass from Mr Todd, then walked Stink along the corridor and round the corner to the nurse's office. Stink pointed to the skeleton in the corner.

"Pretend he's not there, Stink. Sit on the edge of the bed. I'll be the doctor while we wait for Mrs Bell. So, what seems to be the problem?"

"When I woke up this morning, I just had hiccups and a loose tooth. Now my throat hurts."

Judy picked up a flashlight from the desk and shone it in Stink's eyes.

"Hey, now my eyes hurt too!"

"Does your face hurt?"

"Nope."

"It's killing me!" Judy cracked herself up. "Let's see your throat." She shone the light down his throat. "Say ahh!"

"Glub!" said Stink.

"Not *glub*. *Ahhhhh!* Try again."

"Slug!"

"Never mind," said Judy.

"What's wrong?"

"Well, you DON'T have a frog in your throat. Just a glub and a slug." Judy held her head sideways, thinking. She looked Stink up and down.

"Do you have a pain in your neck too?" asked Stink.

"Just you," said Judy. She cracked herself up some more. "Wait a minute! Stink! I got it! I know what you have!"

"What?" asked Stink.

"Skeleton-itis!" said Judy. "Fear-of-Skeletons disease. Found only in second graders with glubby slugs in their throats."

"I can't help it. He just stares ... with those eyes! It's creepier than that pyramid eye on a one-dollar bill."

"Stink, skeletons don't have eyes."

"I know! Just big spooky holes like dead people. And he's all clickety-clackety."

Judy picked up the skeleton from where he was hanging in the corner. "Hi! I'm Mr Dry-Bones!" Judy clacked the skeleton's jaw open and shut. "You can call me George. See? He teaches you about your bones and stuff." Judy made the skeleton wave at Stink.

Stink did not wave back. "You're giving me goose pimples. Put him back before we get in trouble."

"Not till he tells some jokes. Here, I'll practise some jokes I'm learning for my Human Body project. Mr Dry-Bones likes jokes, don't you?" Judy said to the skeleton. "They tickle his *funny bone!*"

Stink cracked up.

"What does a skeleton take for a cold?" asked Judy.

"What?"

"Coffin drops!"

Stink laughed at that one.

"What do skeletons put on their mashed potatoes?"

"Umm..."

"Grave-y! What do you call a skeleton who sleeps all day?"

"Sleepyhead?"

"Lazybones!" Judy cackled. "How does a skeleton pass his maths test?"

"How?"

"He bones up on his addition and subtraction."

"Fun-ny!" Stink laughed and laughed. He seemed to forget all about his sore throat. And Fear-of-Skeletons disease.

"What does a skeleton eat for breakfast?" asked Mrs Bell, setting her handbag down on the desk.

"I don't know. What?"

"Dreaded wheat!"

"Good one!" said Stink. He held his stomach, he was laughing so hard.

"I see you've met George," said Mrs Bell.

"I had to go to another school this morning. So it's just my *skeleton* crew here today."

"Hey, that's good!" said Judy. "I was just, um, helping Stink till you got here."

"Old Mr Dry-Bones is very *humerus*," said Mrs Bell. She cracked herself up. "*Humerus.* That's the name of this long bone right here in your upper arm."

"Cool beans!" said Judy.

"Oh, I get it now!" said Stink, cracking up too.

"See, Stink? I told you he wasn't scary."

"Don't worry," Mrs Bell said to Stink. "Lots of people find bones scary. Did you know even elephants are afraid of bones?"

"Really?" asked Stink.

"Bones are interesting, really. We start out with over three hundred bones when we're born, and when we grow up we have—"

"Only two hundred and six!" said Judy. "We just learnt that in Mr Todd's class."

"How do we lose so many bones?" asked Stink.

"Some grow together," said Mrs Bell. "To hold us up and make us strong. Otherwise we'd all be jellyfish. A jellyfish has no bones."

Judy went all limp, imitating a jellyfish. "See, Stink. Aren't you glad you're not a jellyfish?"

"No, because if I were, I could sting you!"

"So what seems to be the problem, young man?" Mrs Bell asked Stink.

"I have a stomach ache."

"A stomach ache?" said Judy. "I thought you had a sore throat."

"I do. But now my stomach hurts from laughing."

"So I guess you could say your sister had you in *stitches*, huh?"

"Don't give her any ideas!" said Stink.

"Let's just take a look at that throat," said Mrs Bell. "Say *ahh*!"

"AHH!" said Stink.

"Hey! You didn't say *glub*. Or *slug*," said Judy.

"Uh-oh," said Mrs Bell. "Somebody's sick, all right."

"For real?" Judy asked. "Can I see?"

"His throat is as red as a fire engine." Mrs Bell took Stink's temperature with a non-cat-hairy thermometer. "And he has a temperature: 99.9."

"Stink, you have ALL the luck," said Judy.

Majorly Delicious!

No fair! Stink got to go to the real doctor. Judy convinced her mum that she had to come too, so she could learn stuff.

Dr McCavity looked in Stink's eyes and ears and down his throat with a purple tongue depressor. She explained how tonsils are two pink balls like grapes at the back of your throat, and they can get infected with white specks and swell up and hurt.

Dr McCavity told Mrs Moody to give

Stink some special medicine and make sure he got lots of sleep. She told Stink to drink ginger ale and eat the BRAT diet.

"He's been eating the brat diet since he was born!" Judy said.

Dr McCavity laughed. "BRAT means Bananas, Rice, Apple sauce and Toast." She also told Stink to stay home from school till his temperature had gone down, and stay away from Judy as much as possible.

She really did say the last part!

"Just think," Judy told Stink. "If you get tonsillitis, you get to go to the hospital for an operation and get a bracelet with your name on it and wear funny pyjamas and eat Popsicles all day."

"Well, let's hope it doesn't come to that,"

said Mum. "That would be a lot of Popsicles."

"We don't like to take out healthy tonsils," said the doctor.

"But you said they were grapefruits," said Judy. "Maybe he has Grapefruit-itis!"

"Grapes," said Dr McCavity. "Not grapefruit. If he takes care of those tonsils, he won't have to worry about Grapefruit-itis." She laughed again.

"Dr McCavity, you should have been a dentist!" Judy cracked herself up.

"You like jokes? What did the doctor say to the patient with tonsillitis?"

"What?"

"Have a *swell* time!" said Dr McCavity.

@ @ @

Double no fair! Stink got to stay home from school (for real), drink ginger ale (for breakfast) and eat mashed-banana toast all day (the bratty diet). AND he got to watch TV in his room, even though Dr McCavity had not said one thing about TV in your room.

Judy did not stay away from Stink as much as possible.

She took his temperature (way too high) and made him a hospital bracelet with his name (Stinker) on it. She let him use her crazy straw to drink ginger ale. She read him Dr Rex Morgan comics and Cherry Ames, Student Nurse, mysteries.

She wrote him a prescription on her doctor pad.

Stink Moody
Take two Popsicles and
Call me in the morning.
Dr Judy Moody

She even took a Hippopotamus oath to be nice to Stink. Nicey-nice. *Doctor* nice.

"Stink," she said, raising her right hand, "I swear by Neopolitan and Hygiene and Larry Lasagna that I will do everything I can to the best of my ability to help make you better. Here. Pet Mouse." She plopped Mouse on Stink's stomach.

"Ow!" said Stink. "She clawed me!" Mouse jumped to the floor.

Judy picked up Mouse again. "Stink, you have to pet her twenty times. It's called Paws for Healing. It will lower your blood pressure. Trust me."

"Are you sure it's not called Paws for Scratching?"

"Stink. Just try it." Judy plopped her cat on Stink again. Mouse bolted off the bed, knocking over the glass of ginger ale.

"Ahh! Ginger ale! It's all over me!" cried Stink.

Judy got Stink a towel. And a new ginger ale. And a clean crazy straw. She got

him a not-wet blanket. She got him Baxter
and Ebert, his stuffed-animal
penguin and timber wolf.

For four days, she fed Toady. For four days,
she brought Stink his homework. For four
days, she watched *Megazoid and the Deltoid
Bananas* with Stink, even though she
wanted to watch the Operation Channel.

That was when she saw it. In a TV ad
not prescribed by Dr McCavity. The one-
and-only, for-sure cure for Stink.

"Are you tired all the time?"

Yes. Stink was sleeping right now!

"Are you sick? Want to be healthy? Live longer?"

Yes, yes, and YES!! Judy told the TV.

"We have a secret just for you. PRUNES!" said the cartoon lady on TV.

"PRUNES?" cried Judy. "UCK!"

"Bite them, chew them, don't pooh-pooh them," said the TV lady. "CALIFORNIA PRUNES! The energy-packed super snack. Majorly delicious! Off to climb Mount Everest? Take some PRUNES with you today."

Judy did not think Stink would be climbing Mount Everest any time soon. He could barely climb out of bed. But it was worth a try. All she had to do was convince Stink to eat one prune.

Judy tiptoed downstairs and opened the

kitchen cupboards. Tea bags, peanut butter, pretzels, crackers... They had to be here somewhere. Judy pulled a chair over to the up-high cupboards. A-ha! A shiny bag!

Gravy?!

Gravy did not help you climb Mount Everest. Gravy did not cure tonsils. Gravy did not make you live longer.

She spotted a yellow sun shining on the front of a pink and purple bag. Finally! Judy stared at two shrivelled lumps. Prunes were icky. Sticky. Prunes were wrinkly as elephants and looked like one-hundred-and-fifty-year-old buffalo droppings. Two-hundred-year-old dried-up belly buttons. Two-hundred-and-fifty-year-old tonsils. Why did you have to eat bad stuff for good stuff to happen?

The world was backwards, according to Judy Moody.

Dr Judy went back upstairs. "Stink! Wake up!" said Judy.

"Wha...?"

"I have your cure! Right here in my hand. No more fever. No more grapefruit tonsils." Judy held out her hand. She showed Stink the prunes.

"What? What are those?" asked Stink.

"Prunes. The secret to not getting sick. The secret to climbing Mount Everest."

"They look like moon rocks. Or petrified prune rocks."

"They do kind of look like the owl pellets we had in Science…"

"Owl pellets! Owl pellets are hair balls. Owl pellets are vomit."

"Prunes are just plums," said Judy. "C'mon. One bite."

"No way, Prunella de Vil. I am not eating a hair ball. I am not eating vomit."

"Don't you want to live longer? Don't you want to have teeny-tiny tonsils again?"

"OK. Then help me. Say nice things about prunes," said Stink.

Judy sniffed a prune. "They don't smell like buffalo droppings."

"That's the nicest thing you can say about a prune?"

"They're not hairy."

"Not hairy is good," said Stink.

"I know," said Judy. "Close your eyes. On the count of three, we'll BOTH eat a prune at the same time.

"One, one thousand..."

Stink closed his eyes tight.

"Two, one thousand..."

Judy threw her prune in the bin.

"Three—"

Stink actually put the prune in his mouth.

"Eee-yew!" cried Stink. *Thwaaa!* Stink spat out the prune. It went flying across the floor and landed in a dust ball. "I licked it! It touched my taste buds!"

"It's supposed to taste MAJORLY delicious. The TV said so," Judy told him.

"It tastes majorly disgusting," said Stink. "You tricked me!"

"I was just trying to help you feel better," said Judy. "Now I'm a bad doctor and you'll *never* feel better."

"I feel better knowing I'm not going to eat that prune."

"Stink, don't you get it? That was the last prune. Now it has cat hair and spit all over it. What are we going to do?" Before you could say "majorly dust ball", Mouse pounced on the cat-hairy spat-out prune.

"No! Mouse! Wait!" said Judy.

It was too late. *Ga-loomp!* Mouse chewed it up and swallowed. Hair ball, spit and all. Judy and Stink fell on the floor laughing.

Prune Lips licked her paws, face and whiskers.

"Mouse," said Judy, picking up her cat, "you are going to live a very long life."

"*Nine* long lives," said Stink.

Medical Doctor

Doctor Day! The day Judy got to dress up like Elizabeth Blackwell, First Woman Doctor, and do a REAL LIVE operation for Class 3T. An operation was the best of all the brainstorms from her list. The best Human Body project ever. Better even than trying to doctor Stink.

Her patient was special. Her patient had green skin and did *not* talk back. Her patient would not hog the TV and drink all the ginger ale and spit out healthy prunes.

Her patient was perfect. She could hardly wait.

First she took one more bath.

Stink knocked on the bathroom door. "Knock, knock!"

"Who's there?"

"Stink, minus one belly button."

No answer.

"Mum! Judy's hogging the bathroom and she already took a million baths yesterday." Stink banged on the door. "Hurry up! I need to get in there!"

Judy came out with a towel on her head, and all-wrinkly hands and feet. "I liked it better when you were ill," said Judy.

"I liked it better when you didn't look like a spat-out prune," said Stink.

"Doctors have to be really, really clean, Stink. Elizabeth Blackwell took three cold showers a day!"

"Elizabeth Blackwell didn't leave a lake on the floor."

"Hardee-har-har."

"'Hip bone's connected to da leg bone,'" Judy sang as she got dressed. Today was going to be the amazing-est Human Body day ever, from head to toe.

At school, Judy had ants in her pants all through Spelling, bees in her *patella*-knees all through Maths. At last it was Science. Mr Todd said the magic words. "Time for our Human Body projects. Rocky, why don't you go first?"

Rocky wrapped himself in toilet paper like a mummy, and told how eating a mummy can help your tummy! No lie. Doctors in the old-old-olden days thought mummies could cure stuff like stomach aches. So they ground up mummies, bones and all, and used them for medicine.

"Creepy!" said most of the class.

"Fascinating," said Judy.

Jessica Finch wrote *medi-words*

on the board. Words like *intelligirl* (really smart girl), *brainiac* (has super-Einstein, not-kidney-bean brain) and *brain case* (sick in the brain), which she added to the dictionary. Then she passed out a word search. Judy found all the *medi-words* at *brainiac* speed.

Finally, Mr Todd called on her. Dr Judy Elizabeth Blackwell. She put on her doctor shirt, a stethoscope and a left-eye patch. She taped plastic bags over her shoes. She coloured between her eyebrows with a black marker and stuck fake bugs on her head with tape. "Today I am Elizabeth Blackwell, First Woman Doctor," said Judy. "I'll start with a poem." She took a deep

breath, so she wouldn't get a terrible case of nerves. Or a bad case of sweat.

"Elizabeth Blackwell

Lived in an attic
Nothing was automatic

First in her class
What more could you ask?

Became first woman doctor
Even though boys mocked her

Opened a clinic
Helped poor people in it

Delivered babies
Gave shots for rabies (maybe)

Opened her own school
It was way cool

Wrote a book
Wonder how long it took

Born, I don't know when
Died, 1910

Take after the example
Of Dr Elizabeth Blackwell."

Everybody clapped. "Any questions before I begin the operation?" Judy asked.

"Why are you wearing pyjamas?" asked Hailey.

"Scrubs," said Judy. "It's a doctor shirt. Doctors have to be really, really clean and take tons of baths a day."

"Why do you only have one eyebrow?" asked Frank.

"It's a uni-brow. Like Elizabeth Blackwell had. Plus it makes me look intelligent. Like an *intelligirl* who is not a *brain case*."

"Why do you have that pirate patch on your eye?" asked Brad.

"Elizabeth Blackwell got an eye infection and they took out her eye, so she wore an eye patch."

"Ooh. Gross!"

"Why do you have fake bugs on your head?" asked Jessica Finch.

"They didn't really know how to fix her eye, so they put bloodsucking leeches on her head. They thought it would help."

"EEE-yew!" said a bunch of kids in the class.

"Did you write that poem?"

"Well, it wasn't a gnome!"

"Why do you have plastic bags on your feet?"

"In case of blood," said Judy.

"Class, let's let Judy show us her project," said Mr Todd.

"Time for a real live operation!" said Judy.

"Do it on me!" said Frank.

"Not me!" said Rocky.

"If you need a guinea pig," said Jessica Finch, "do it on Peanut."

"I already have a patient."

"Is it dead?" asked Brad.

"My patient is alive, not dead. My patient is better to practise on than a little brother. My patient has lots of guts. Ooey-gooey guts."

"Who is it?"

"Tell us!"

"Does it have a name?"

"Yes."

"Oh no! Does it have green skin?" asked Rocky.

"Yes!" said Judy.

"It's Toady!" Frank called out.

"Her name is … Ima," said Judy. She held up a zucchini with a Magic-Marker face. "Ima Green Zucchini!"

The whole class clapped.

Frank came up front to help. He held up Judy's X-ray drawing of the insides of a zucchini. "First, make sure you take an X-ray, so you know what you're doing."

"What's that big black blob?" asked Rocky.

"That's the thing I'm going to remove.

The appendix. Nobody really knows what the appendix is for, so it's a good thing to take out."

"I had my appendix out," said Alison S.

"I had mine out twice," said Brad.

"Before you start," said Judy, "don't forget to take the Hippo oath. Swear by the Hippo guy, Father of Medicine, and Mr Clean and Louis Lasagna that you will do your doctor best. Then make sure the patient is clean."

Judy turned to Frank. "Toothbrush!" She scrubbed the zucchini with a toothbrush.

"Needle." Frank handed her the needle from her doctor kit.

"Give the patient a shot, so they fall asleep. Use your nicey-nicey voice and tell them they won't feel a thing. Or tell them a joke to make them feel OK. Like, what vegetable lives in a cage? A *zoo-chini!*"

Frank cracked up the most at that one.

"Knife!" Frank handed Judy a plastic knife.

"Next, make the incision."

"I-N-C-I-S-I-O-N," said Intelligirl Jessica Finch, Queen of Medi-words. "A cut, slash or gash."

Judy poked the zucchini with the plastic knife.

"Scissors," said Judy. Frank handed her the scissors.

Snip, snip, snip.

"Blood!" Judy said to Frank. She pointed to the ketchup bottle. Frank poured ketchup all over the zucchini.

"Operations have lots of blood."

"All this ketchup stuff is making me hungry for hot dogs and stuff," said Rocky.

"Tweezers!" She whispered "Clothes peg" to Frank.

"Take out the appendix." Judy pulled out a hunk of seeds with the clothes peg.

"Sponge!" Judy picked up the zucchini and wiped off the ketchup-blood. The zucchini was so ketchup-y, it slipped out of Judy's hands and fell to the floor.

OH NO!

The kids in 3T leant out of their seats to see what had happened. There, in the middle of the aisle, was perfect patient Ima Green Zucchini, lying in a pool of ketchup-blood, broken in two!

"Rule number one: stay calm," said Judy. "Admit 'I know not' what to do!"

Then she had an idea. Judy picked up both halves of her patient and said to Frank, "Sutures!" So Frank handed her a needle and some thread.

"I'll just sew the patient back up." Judy showed the class how to make nice neat stitches. *In, out, in, out.*

"Don't just do a *sew-sew* job. Or your patient will have a purple Frankenstein scar. Or a pizza-shaped scar, like mine." Judy pulled up her sleeve to show her own bumpy pizza-scar, from the time she fell over chasing the ice-cream van. Judy and Frank laughed till their appendixes hurt.

Frank helped Judy put Band-Aids all

over her patient. "Wait one week, then take the stitches out. Tell them to rest and eat prunes and plenty of Screamin' Mimi's ice cream. No, wait. That's for tonsils. Whatever! The end."

Everybody clapped really hard. "Good job," said Mr Todd. "Nice details. You really thought of everything. I'd say it was a *smashing* success!"

Medical Disaster

The very next day after Operation Zucchini, Frank Pearl brought a cardboard person to school. A cardboard person that looked exactly like him.

"Awesome," said Rocky. "You have a twin!"

"He's my clone. I'm Frank. He's Stein. Get it? We're Frank-and-Stein!"

Judy hoped Frank-and-Stein was not better than Operation Zucchini.

Frank Pearl told the class how you get DNA from a bone or a hair. "One cell has all your genes. You can make another one of you, exactly like you, by cloning. You can't see your genes," said Frank. "But it's all there."

"I can see my jeans. I'm wearing them," said Brad.

"Not jeans that you wear. G-E-N-E, genes. DNA is the stuff that makes you YOU."

"Cool beans," said Judy.

"Scientists cloned a sheep and named her Dolly. And they cloned a bunch of mice. And some pigs, right here in Virginia," Frank told the class.

"Is that true, Mr Todd?" asked Jessica Finch.

"It's science fiction," said Alison S.

"Like *Jurassic Park*," said Rocky.

"It's true," said Mr Todd.

"They found a mammoth frozen in ice and they might try to clone it with DNA so mammoths won't be extinct any more. No lie," said Frank.

"Thank you, Frank," said Mr Todd. "Very interesting. Most of us just think of cloning as science fiction."

❧   ❧   ❧

The rest of the morning, Frank Pearl did not pay attention once. Judy wrote him a note, but he didn't write back. She told him a joke, but he didn't laugh.

"Frank! What's wrong?" Judy asked.

"My project was no good."

"Was so!" said Judy. "You're a gene-ius."

"My project was cardboard. *Dead* cardboard. Nobody even believes it's real. Yours had something real. Something alive." He just stared at Peanut, the dwarf guinea pig.

"Why are you staring at Peanut?" asked Judy.

"I was just thinking how she must be lonely all by herself," said Frank.

"Judy, Frank, are you with us?" asked Mr Todd.

"Sorry, Mr Todd," said Judy. "Frank's worried about Peanut. Do guinea pigs get lonely? For friends?"

"Yes, well, guinea pigs do enjoy company."

"I have guinea pigs, and my guinea-pig book says you're never supposed to have just one guinea pig," said Jessica Finch.

"That's why we take turns playing with her every day," said Mr Todd. "And we made her a fun box, remember? Now let's keep our minds on our work, OK?"

🌀 🌀 🌀

At morning recess, Frank found Judy and Rocky at the water fountain. "You guys have to help me get in trouble," said Frank.

"Are you crazy?" asked Rocky.

"Do you *want* to go to Antarctica?" Judy asked Frank.

"No, I just want Mr Todd to make me stay inside during lunch recess. I need to try a science experiment. A real one. About cloning."

"Cool beans," said Rocky.

"Cool genes," said Judy, cracking herself up. "What kind of experiment?"

"Cloning Peanut. I'll make another guinea pig exactly like her. Right here in Class 3T. So she'll have a friend. Or *friends*. Real ones, not cardboard. If it works, nobody will think cloning is just science fiction."

"Cloning just works on aliens," said Rocky.

"And bones. And frozen stuff," Judy said.

"Nah-uh," said Frank.

"Well, it's against the law to practise science on animals. Stink told me. You have to use a zucchini or something."

"Everybody clones vegetables. And does experiments on *zucchinis*."

"What's wrong with that? Real doctors practise stitches on zucchinis. It's way scientific."

"Cloning a guinea pig is way MORE scientific."

"Get real!" said Judy. "You can't just be a cloner. You need equipment. Fancy stuff, like scientists have. In labs."

"It's easy. All I need is DNA (a few hairs from Peanut), a Petri dish like Rocky used for Lego germs, and electricity. Plus a little help from you guys."

"DNA means *Do Not Ask* me to experiment on animals!" said Judy. "I'll watch, but only to make sure you don't hurt Peanut."

"Let's ask Mr Todd if we can stay inside at recess and clean Peanut's cage," said Frank. "Then nobody gets in trouble."

"Perfect," said Rocky.

"Genius," said Judy.

"Scientific," said Frank, tapping a finger to his head.

෧   ෧   ෧

When the lunch bell rang, Judy, Rocky and Frank stayed inside. They lined the bottom of Peanut's cage with clean newspaper and straw. They filled up her water bottle.

They gave her a new, never-been-chewed toilet-paper tube to hide in.

As soon as Mr Todd left to get his lunch, Frank said, "Quick!" He got Mr Todd's pointy scissors. Rocky held Peanut while Frank went *snip, snip, snip.*

"Be careful," said Judy. "I'm watching."

"Haircuts don't hurt!" said Frank. He carefully placed four hairs in the Petri dish. "All we need now is electricity."

"How about the microwave?" said Rocky.

Frank put the guinea-pig hairs in the microwave. "Three minutes," he said, pressing the buttons.

"I'll say some magic words," said Rocky. "Let me think. How's this:

"Snip of hair, electric power.
How many guinea pigs per hour?
Eeny meany, dead Houdini.
Two, ten, twelve, fourteeny."

Ding! Frank took out the Petri dish and put it back in Peanut's cage.

"Hide it under some straw," said Rocky.

"Now what do we do?" asked Judy.

"Wait," said Frank.

"This will never work," said Judy. "You should have practised on a zucchini."

❧   ❧   ❧

The next morning, when Judy got to school, Frank was looking in Peanut's cage. Nothing! No more guinea pigs. Not two. Not ten. Not fourteeny. Just Peanut, sleeping with her head on a lettuce pillow.

"It didn't work. Cloning must be harder than I thought," said Frank.

"Told you," said Judy.

"I'm not giving up," said Frank. "Everybody knows science takes time."

They waited some more. On Thursday and Friday, when Judy got to school Frank was already there, standing over Peanut's cage. Nothing. Zip. Zero-teeny.

Peanut was alone. Un-cloned. Frank Pearl was having Double Trouble.

❧ ❧ ❧

Then, on Monday morning, it happened. While Judy was doodling guinea-pig clones with her Grouchy pencil and waiting for the school bell to ring, somebody yelled, "Hey! Peanut has a friend!"

Judy dropped her Grouchy pencil. She rushed over to Peanut's cage. Peanut *did* have a friend. No lie! For real and absolute positive! Not one friend, but one-two-three-four friends! One clone for every hair Frank had snipped.

"SCIENCE RULES!" Frank shouted.

"What happened?"

"Where did all these guinea pigs come from?"

"I cloned Peanut!" Frank told the class. "At first it didn't work. Then *presto*! Four guinea pigs! Double-triple-quadruple Frank-and-Stein magic!"

"They're not clones! Kids can't clone stuff."

"Are they real?"

"Did Peanut have babies?"

Judy Moody blinked once, twice, three times. She could not believe her retinas, irises or pupils. Frank Pearl had cloned Peanut the dwarf guinea pig! She saw it with her own eyeballs. Eyeballs did not lie.

"I did it! I cloned Peanut. I'm a world-famous kid scientist! The youngest person ever to clone a guinea pig!" shouted Frank.

"I helped!" said Judy. "Don't forget me, Judy Moody, First Girl Doctor. We did it together – right, Frank? We're both famous. I bet I – I mean *we* – will be in *The Guinness Book of Records. Ripley's Believe It or Not!*"

"Or NOT!" said one-two-three voices. Three annoying, not-funny, used-to-be-friends voices.

Frank laughed so hard he made spit fly. Rocky sprayed her too. Worst of all, Jessica Finch was laughing her *medulla* off! She jumped up and down saying, "They're mine, they're mine, they're all my guinea

pigs. Chester had babies and we played a trick on YOU, Judy Moody!"

"You fell for it," said Frank.

"You swallowed it like a pill," said Rocky.

What was she thinking? She, Judy Moody, was not First Girl Doctor, first to help clone a guinea pig. It was all a joke. A trick. A big fat bunch of clone-y baloney.

"You should see your face!" said Rocky.

"We were just *cloning* around," said Frank.

"Did you really think you *cloned* a *guinea pig*?" asked Jessica.

"Of course not," said Judy. She searched under the straw and pulled out the Petri dish. Still there. It now had four hairs, eight, sixteen, thirty-two... The only things that had multiplied were guinea-pig hairs.

"Ha ha! Yes, you did!" said Jessica Finch.

Judy's blood pressure went up. Her temperature was rising! She, Judy Moody, felt as silly as Bozo the Clone.

"Meet Jasmine, Cindy, Coco and Nutmeg," said Jessica. "The Spice Girls."

"The Not-Nice girls! And boys," she said, looking at Rocky and Frank. "Mr Todd's going to be here any minute. Don't you need to go and sit down or something?"

"Yes," said Frank. "To write a letter to *Ripley's Believe It or Not!* 'Dear Mr Ripley: Believe it or not, we played the best-joke-ever on our friend Judy Moody.'"

"ROAR!" said Judy.

Mumpty Dumpty

The next morning, Judy Moody woke up sick. Not fake sick. Not just mad-at-her-friends sick. Really and truly sick. Pain-in-the-brain sick. Hot-in-the-head sick. Frog-in-the-throat sick.

Judy ran to the mirror and stuck out her tongue. It was red, all right. Not just Cherry-Ames-cough-drop red. Fire-engine red! And she saw a bumpy, mumps-of-a-lump in the back of her throat – one on each side. She, Judy Moody, had grapefruit tonsils. Bowling-ball tonsils!

The lumps made her look like a hound dog. The lumps made her look like a clone of Peanut-the-dwarf-guinea-pig (with chipmunk cheeks). The lumps made her look like Mumpty Dumpty.

Dad came into her room. He felt her forehead. He looked in her Lumpty-Dumpty throat. He took her temperature.

"You're sick, all right," said Dad, peering at the thermometer. "Looks just like what Stink had. Must be tonsillitis."

Stink came into her room before leaving for school to see if she was sick for real.

"Stink!" Judy whisper-yelled. "Get out of my room!" The lumps made her sound funny.

"Get off your broom?"

"My *room*. Get out."

"How come?"

"You don't want to catch a bad case of lumps!"

Mouse jumped up onto the bottom bunk.

"How come Mouse gets to be in there and I don't?"

"Cats don't have tonsils!"

"Stink, don't get too close to Judy!" yelled Mum.

Stink was not allowed in her room! RARE!

Staying at home sick was not as fun as Judy thought it would be. When Mum brought ginger ale with a crazy straw, it went up Judy's nose. When Dad brought toast with mashed bananas, Judy took one look and said, "I think somebody already ate this." And, worst of all, TV shows in the middle of the day were full of kissing.

Mum took Judy's temperature for real, with a brand-new, no-cat-hair therm-ometer. Human temperature: 101.9! "I called Dr McCavity," said Mum. "This will make you feel better." She held out some medicine. Not double-yum baby aspirin that tastes like orange sweets and that you get to chew. Not triple-yum cough medicine

 that tastes like grape sweets and that you get to drink. A pill! Not just any old pill. A big pill. A monster pill. A pill the size of Nebraska.

Mum wanted her to swallow it. Not chew it. Not drink it. Swallow it. Mum wanted her to swallow Nebraska!

Judy held her throat. "I can't swallow," she said in a sickly way.

"You were swallowing ginger ale just fine," said Mum.

"Ginger ale is not Nebraska!" Judy mumbled in her bowling-ball-tonsils voice. Her words came out all mumbly-dumbly.

"Alaska?" said Mum.

"Ne-bras-ka!" said Judy.

"Just try," said Mum. "It will make you feel lots better."

Judy shut her eyes. She pinched her nose, put the pill in her mouth and gulped down a glass of water.

"That's better," said Mum. Judy stuck out her tongue. The pill was still there!

"Judy, how are you going to be a doctor if you can't take your own medicine?"

"When I'm a doctor, I'll invent a pill-swallowing machine," said Judy.

"OK. Never mind. I'll crush it up and you can drink it."

"Wang hoo," said Judy.

@ @ @

Judy felt lousy. Lousier than lice. Lumpier than mumps. Germier than worms.

A day without school was longer than a month. A day without school took a year. But at least she, Bozo the Clone, did not have to go to school and face her not-so-funny friends.

Still, if they made up, she could be passing notes to Rocky right now. Or telling jokes to Frank Pearl. Or making faces at Jessica Rodent-Fink Finch. But they were all at school, school, school. Learning fun, interesting, fascinating, not pain-in-the-brain stuff, like the smallest bone in your ear is an *ossicle* (not Popsicle). Or how to spell *maxilla* (a jawbone, not Godzilla).

Judy wished she could clone a friend to have right here, right now. Instead, she counted Band-Aids in her Band-Aid collection. Three hundred thirty-seven. Plus thirteen on Hedda-Get-Betta, her doctor doll. Plus a brand-new box of thirty bug Band-Aids she got from Mum this morning just for being ill!

337 + 13 + 30 = too hard to figure out when you're not at school.

She practised her signature, fast and messy like real doctors.

She drew cartoons on her pillowcase with markers. Frank with a moustache. Rocky with Frankenstein hair. Jessica Finch with a rodent brain. A Stink spider's web.

She made a list of all her stuffed animals.

Ned Bear
Ted Bear
Fred Bear
Cornflake (not-cloned Guinea pig)
Brownie
Tookie (Toucan)
Snowflake (Loon from Minnesota)
Auggie ←
Doggie
Pepper (smells like pepper)

There were more, but writing them all down gave her writer's cramp on top of bowling-ball tonsils.

She took her own temperature. With the fancy thermometer that beeped. It was not normal. It was not 98.6. Judy's temperature was 188.8! Judy's temperature was

00.0! Judy's temperature was *beep-beep-beep-beep-beep*. She, Judy Moody, had the temperature of an outer-space alien!

She stared at cracks in the ceiling. The Big Dipper. A giant hot dog. A brain (without a pain in it).

Judy took her temperature again. *Beeeeeeep!* Still 00.0.

"Mouse, stick out your tongue," she said. She held the thermometer under Mouse's tongue. Mouse's temperature was  ... the letter *M*. She tried again. Mouse's temperature was *ERR*. Mouse's temperature was not even numbers. Mouse's temperature was not even human. Mouse the cat was sicker than she, Dr Judy Moody!

"Poor baby!" said Judy. She fed Mouse an ABC (*Already Been Chewed*) mashed-banana toast strip. Mouse loved mashed bananas.

She speed-read one of Stink's Megazoid books about evil ants from an asteroid between Mars and Jupiter that try to take over the universe.

She read two days of Dr Rex Morgan comics Dad had saved for her. She read three chapters of a Cherry Ames, Student Nurse, mystery till her eyes felt ker-flooey.

Finally, after about a hundred years, Stink came home from school. After about a hundred more years, he came upstairs and walked right into her room.

"Stink! Worms! Worms are everywhere. You better get out of here."

"Worms?"

"Germs, Stink. Germs! Didn't you see the sign?" Judy pointed to the sign she had made on the door. "*QUARANTINE! That means STAY AWAY!*"

"Mum said to bring you your homework. Plus I brought other stuff."

"Like what?"

"A wooden nickel from Rocky. That he got from Suzie the Magic Lady. It has a picture of a rabbit coming out of a hat."

"I'm mad at him," said Judy. "In fact, I'm smad. And I'm not going to make up for a nickel. Wooden or not."

"Here's a card from Jessica Finch, with a pretend spelling quiz. See?" The card said:

"And you have to look inside for the right answer."

Judy opened the card. It said:

"I think she meant to put *Your Un-pal, Jessica Finch.*"

"And – da-da da-DA! – a love note from Frank Pearl," Stink told her.

"Give me that," said Judy.

"I made you something at school today too." Stink took a mashed-up wad of paper out of his backpack.

"A mashed-up wad of paper?" said Judy. "Sank woo very much."

"N-O! It's a cootie catcher! I can catch germs with it. See?" Stink jumped up and down, grabbing at air.

"Stink!" said Judy. "Don't make me waff."

"OK, OK. I won't make you waff. But look. It tells fortunes." Stink held out the cootie catcher. "Pick a number."

Judy looked at the cootie catcher. She could not find a number. All she could find were funny-looking words.

"It's French!" said Stink. "We learnt French colours and numbers today. Pick one." Judy pointed to *quatre*. "Four," said Stink. "*Un, deux, trois, quatre.* Now pick a colour."

"If you say so," said Judy. She pointed to *bleu*. It looked like *blue* with the letters mixed up.

"Blue. B-L-E-U," said Stink. "Pick one more colour."

Judy pointed to another one.

"Red. R-O-U-G-E," said Stink. He lifted up the flap.

"Here's your fortune," said Stink. *"Il y a un dragon dans mon lit."*

"What's that mean?" asked Judy. "Your friends are a bunch of clone-y baloneys?"

"It means *There's a dragon in my bed*," Stink told her.

"That's it? That's my fortune?"

"It's that or *My horse is dizzy*," said Stink. "Those are the only two sentences I learnt so far."

"I know one more," said Judy.

"You know French?" asked Stink.

"*Oui*," said Judy. She took out her doctor pad. She wrote a prescription for Stink.

Stink Moody
Get out of my room-ay
and close-ay le door-ay!
Dr Judy Moody

Most Definitely

She, Judy Moody, was in a mood. A sick-of-being-sick mood. Even her bowling-ball pyjamas didn't cheer her up. They made her think of tonsils. Judy put on her around-the-world postcard pyjamas.

Dr McCavity told Mum that Judy might not feel like herself again for about twelve days.

Twelve days! Her human temperature was rising just thinking about it! Her blood pressure was skyrocketing! Twelve days before she could stop talking like a cat underwater. Twelve days before she could learn any new bones or spell *scapula* or stay away from Antarctica.

Twelve more days to feel like Bozo the Clone.

Judy made up a song: "The Twelve Days of Tonsils".

On the first day of tonsils
My brother gave to me
one cootie catcher
And a love note from Frank P.

That was as far as she got before falling asleep. Again. She slept all through the second day of tonsils.

Tonsils, Day 3: Judy drew an X-ray of her

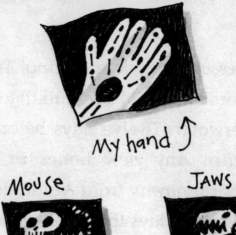

My hand ↑

Mouse

JAWS ↘

Ned
Bear →

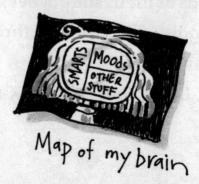

SMARTS | Moods
OTHER STUFF

Map of my brain

hand; an X-ray of Mouse; an X-ray of Jaws, her Venus flytrap; and one of Ned Bear.

Tonsils, Day 4: Back to Dr McCavity.

Tonsils, Day 5: BOR-ing! Judy drew a map of her brain.

Tonsils, Day 6: When she became a doctor, she would find a cure for fire-engine tonsils so sick people did not have to make X-rays of cats and maps of their brains all day.

Tonsils, Day 7: *Ding-dong!* Maybe Stink was home from school. Judy crawled back under the covers, put her head under all her stuffed animals and pretended to be asleep.

"Knock, knock," said Stink.

"I'm asleep," said Judy.

"Knock, knock," said Stink again.

"Stink, have you been eating the BRAT diet again?"

"Just say *Who's there*," said Stink.

"Who's there?" asked Judy.

"US!" said Rocky, Frank and Jessica Finch. All three of her UN-best friends!

"What are YOU guys doing here?" Judy grumped. "You came to laugh at my chipmunk cheeks, didn't you? You heard I have bowling-ball tonsils and came to tell me I look like Mumpty Dumpty."

"No!" said Frank. "We—"

"Wait. Let me guess. You cloned an anteater. An armadillo. An aardwolf. Ha ha. Very funny."

"We brought you something to make

up … I mean, we brought you something to make you feel better," said Rocky.

"Nothing will make me feel better," said Judy. "I feel lousy. As in licey. As in not-nicey."

"But this really works," said Frank.

"Is it a pill?" asked Judy. "I hope it's not a pill the size of Nebraska."

"No."

"Is it a prune? I hope it's not a goony old prune."

"Nope."

"Is it a Band-Aid? I hope it *is* a Band-Aid, with words."

"No, no and nope," said Jessica Finch.

"Does it squeak? I hear squeaking!"

"Yes!" said Jessica.

"Does it have fur, fins or fangs?"

"Yes!" said Stink.

Rocky held up a shirt with words.

"A shirt does not have fur or fins or fangs."

"Look," said Frank, turning the shirt over. "We made it for you at Rocky's house." The shirt said PAWS FOR HEALING. It had blue guinea-pig paw prints all over it.

"Hello! A shirt doesn't squeak!" said Judy.

"No," said Rocky. "But pets do. We brought you animals to pet!"

"Just like Paws for Healing," said Frank.

"So you can lower your blood pressure and not feel sick," said Jessica.

Rocky had brought Houdini, his pet iguana. Frank had brought a red and purple fish in a jar, and Jessica Finch had brought Chester and all four of the baby guinea pigs – the (un-cloned) Spice Girls!

Stink went to his room and brought back Toady.

"You brought half the zoo!" said Judy.

"And I got you a real Paws for Healing badge," said Stink. "From the hospital gift shop." He held out a badge that said I'M IN CHARGE OF CRITTER-COOL CARE.

"Cool!" said Frank.

"Critter-cool!" said Judy. She put the Paws for Healing shirt on over her around-the-world postcard pyjamas. She pinned the badge to her shirt.

Rocky held out Houdini. "You hold him, while I clip his toe nails."

Snip, snip, snip.

"He has more toe nails than Stink!" Judy laughed.

Frank set his fish on Judy's desk, next to her jelly bean collection. "My aunt got me this Siamese fighting fish when I was sick. I named her Judy."

"Same-same!" said Judy.

"You can keep her till you get better. I know you can't pet her, but it's supposed to relax you and make you feel better just to watch her."

"I promise I'll watch her all the time," said Judy.

"Look! Judy the Fighting Fish is blowing bubbles!" said Stink.

"Rare!" said the not-fish Judy.

"And you can play with Toady any time you want," said Stink. "As long as you don't operate on him."

"I won't," said Judy. "I promise."

Jessica brought special shampoo, and they each gave a guinea pig a bath. "Coco hates baths," said Jessica. "But guinea pigs have to be clean."

"Just like doctors!" Judy said.

When they were done, they each got to blow-dry their guinea pigs.

"Nutmeg's ready for a party!" said Judy, stroking the guinea pig's fur. Jessica got Cindy to roll over twice, and Coco twitched her whiskers at Cornflake, Judy's stuffed guinea pig.

"That means hello in guinea pig," said Jessica. "She's trying to make friends!" Everybody cracked up.

Nutmeg squirmed out of Judy's arms and ran in circles round her room.

"Uh-oh!" said Jessica. Nutmeg ran round Judy's floor pillow. She ran round Ned Bear, Ted Bear and Fred Bear, the rubbish bin and Judy's doctor kit. She ran round and round Judy's squiggle rug.

"Catch her!" said Stink.

Everybody chased Nutmeg. Even Mouse. Nutmeg hid under Judy's squiggle rug. Jessica caught her with an ice-cream container.

"Phew! That was a close one, girl," said

Judy, rubbing the guinea pig's tummy. "Hey, look! Nutmeg likes tummy rubs!"

"She likes you," said Jessica.

"Aw. I wish I could keep her for ever and ever," said Judy. "I promise not to clone her."

"She's still too young," said Jessica. "But when the Spice Girls get older, my dad says we can take them to the hospital for Paws for Healing. You know, help some more kids feel better."

"RARE!" said Judy.

◎　◎　◎

When everybody had gone home, Judy climbed back under the covers and leant against all her stuffed animals. She was feeling not-so-sick-any-more. Her tonsils did not feel so lumpy. She, Judy Moody, did not feel so grumpy. Friends were better than prunes. Friends were better than medicine. Friends were better than all the ginger ale, ABC toast and TV in the world.

Her temperature was dropping. So was her blood pressure. Her tonsils were shrinking fast. Most definitely!

Judy Moody took out her mood journal. She wrote herself a poem. A moody poem. A Mumpty-Dumpty poem.

Mumpty Dumpty had a great case of lumps.
Mumpty Dumpty hAd a worse case of grumps.
All Judy's brothers and all Judy's friends
Helped put Mumpty back together again.

Judy took out her doctor pad. She, Dr
Judy Moody, wrote *herself* a prescription.

PATIENT: Judy MOody

Hold Houdini. Watch a fish.
Pet a guinea pig. If THAT does
NOT WORK — have fun with three
friends and call me in the morning.
Dr Judy Moody

Last but not least, Judy signed her name
with a scribbly doctor signature.

Dr Judy Moody

10 Things You May Not Know About Megan McDonald

10. The first story Megan ever got published (in the fifth grade) was about a pencil sharpener.

9. She read the biography of Virginia Dare so many times at her school library that the librarian had to ask her to give somebody else a chance.

8. She had to be a boring-old pilgrim every year for Halloween because she has four older sisters, who kept passing their pilgrim costumes down to her.

7. Her favourite board game is the Game of Life.

6. She is a member of the Ice-Cream-for-Life Club at Screamin' Mimi's in her hometown of Sebastopol, California.

5. She has a Band-Aid collection to rival Judy Moody's, including bacon-scented Band-Aids.

4. She owns a jawbreaker that is bigger than a baseball, which she will never, ever eat.

3. Like Stink, she had a pet newt that slipped down the drain when she was his age.

2. She often starts a book by scribbling on a napkin.

1. And the number-one thing you may not know about Megan McDonald is: she was once the opening act for the World's Biggest Cupcake!

10 Things You May Not Know About Peter H. Reynolds

10. He has a twin brother, Paul. Paul was born first, fourteen minutes before Peter decided to arrive.

9. Peter is part owner of a children's book and toy shop called the Blue Bunny in the Massachusetts town where he lives.

8. He's vertically challenged (aka short!).

7. His mother is from England; his father is from Argentina.

6. He made his first animated film while he was in high school.

5. He sometimes paints with tea instead of water – whatever's handy!

4. He keeps a sketch pad and pen on his nightstand. That way, if an idea hits him in the middle of the night, he can jot it down immediately.

3. His favourite candy is a tie between peanut-butter cups and chocolate-covered raisins (same as Megan McDonald!).

2. One of his favourite books growing up was *The Tall Book of Make-Believe* by Jane Werner, illustrated by Garth Williams.

1. And the number-one thing you may not know about Peter H. Reynolds is: he shares a birthday with James Madison, Stink's favourite president!

Have you read them all?

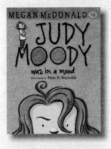

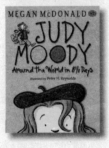

The *whole world's* in a Judy Moody mood!

Say hello to . . .

Fleur Humeur (Judy Moody in the Netherlands)

or Dada Nalada (Judy Moody in Slovakia)

or Hania Humorek (Judy Moody in Poland).

The Judy Moody series has been published in more than twenty countries and languages, for a grand total of more than **16 million books** in print worldwide.

Open up a book – anywhere, anytime – and get ready for your *best mood ever*!

DOUBLE RARE!

Judy Moody has her own interactive website!

Visit **www.judymoody.com** for all things Judy Moody and lots of way-not-boring fun stuff, including:

- The Official Judy Moody Fan Club

- Interactive games and a Mood Meter

- Way-not-boring stuff about Megan McDonald and Peter H. Reynolds

- Digital downloads, including emoticons and wallpapers

- Sample chapters and downloadable reading logs

Judy and Stink are starring together!

Judy Moody and Stink
The Holly Joliday

Judy Moody and Stink
*The Mad, Mad, Mad, Mad
Treasure Hunt*

In full colour!

Be sure to check out Stink's adventures too!

Stink Moody has his own website!
(One he doesn't have to share with his bossy older sister, Judy)

for the latest in all things Stink, visit
www.stinkmoody.com
where you can:

- Test your Stink knowledge with an I.Q. quiz

- Write and illustrate your own comic strip

- Create your own guinea pig: choose its colours, name it and e-mail it to a friend!

- Guess Stink's middle name

- Learn way-not-boring stuff about Megan McDonald and Peter H. Reynolds

- Read the Stink-y fact of the week!